SHANNON
the Ocean
Fairy

Special thanks to
Narinder Dhami

ORCHARD BOOKS
338 Euston Road, London NW1 3BH
Orchard Books Australia
Level 17/207 Kent Street, Sydney, NSW 2000
A Paperback Original

First published in 2008 by Orchard Books.

HIT entertainment

A CIP catalogue record for this book is available
from the British Library.

ISBN 978 1 40830 025 1
9 10 8

Printed in Great Britain

Orchard Books is a division of Hachette Children's Books,
an Hachette Livre UK company

www.hachettelivre.co.uk

SHANNON
the Ocean
Fairy

by Daisy Meadows

ORCHARD

Jack Frost's Ice Castle

Kirsty's Gran's House

Lighthouse

Cruiseliner

Café

ARCADES

Dock

Leamouth Pier

Sealions

The Enchanted Pearl

To the palace we will go,
Because my spell will make it so.
Enchanted Pearls I mean to take,
Leaving chaos in my wake.

Tides will rise to flood both worlds,
While my goblins have the pearls.
So goblins keep them safe for me
Hidden deep beneath the sea.

Contents

Party in Fairyland   11

High Tide   21

Underwater World   33

A Treasure Trail   43

In the Coral Cave   53

Party in Fairyland

"Race you to that rock pool, Kirsty!"
Rachel Walker yelled to her best friend,
Kirsty Tate.

"You're on!" Kirsty replied.

Laughing, the two girls raced across
the beach. Rachel reached the pool first,
but Kirsty was right behind her.

"Your gran's lucky to live in Leamouth," Rachel panted, gazing around the sandy bay. "It's lovely."

Kirsty nodded. Leamouth was a pretty fishing village with winding streets and a harbour filled with boats. Kirsty's gran lived in one of the cottages on the cliff, near the beach.

"I always have fun here," said Kirsty. "I'm glad you could come too, this time."

"Thanks for inviting me," Rachel replied.

The two girls wandered down to the sea. The waves lapped at their flip-flops, but as the water slid back,

it left a large seashell
on the sand, right
in front of them.

Rachel picked
it up. "It's beautiful,"
she said. "Look!"

As Kirsty looked,
a burst of aquamarine
sparkles suddenly fizzed out of the shell,
making Rachel jump.

"Fairy magic!" Kirsty gasped.

The girls glanced excitedly at each
other. Their friendship with the fairies
was a very special secret.

The faint tinkle of bells and soft music
floated out of the shell. Quickly, Rachel
held it up so that she and Kirsty could
listen.

"Hello, girls," said a silvery voice.

13

Rachel grinned at Kirsty. "It's the Fairy Queen!" she exclaimed.

"We'd like to invite you to a special beach party – a luau – to celebrate summer," the Queen went on. "If you'd like to come, just place the shell on the sand, right now. We hope you can join us…" The Queen's voice faded away.

With a quick
glance round to make
sure nobody was watching,
Rachel placed the seashell on
the sand. Immediately, a dazzling
rainbow sprang from the shell,
its colours bright in the sunshine.
"Let's go, Kirsty!" Rachel whispered.
Kirsty nodded, and the girls stepped
onto the rainbow. As soon as they did
so, they were whisked away in a whirl
of fairy magic.

When the sparkles vanished, the girls
realised that they had been magically
transformed into fairies and were now in
Fairyland, standing on a beautiful sandy
beach next to a glittering turquoise sea.

The beach was crowded with fairies enjoying the luau.

As the girls stepped off the rainbow, their fairy friends rushed to greet them, including King Oberon and Queen Titania.

"We're so glad you could come, girls," said the King kindly.

"A party wouldn't be the same without you," the Queen added.

"Thank you for inviting us," Rachel

and Kirsty chorused.
"Come and boogie!"
called Jade the Disco Fairy.
Laughing, Rachel and
Kirsty started dancing with
Jade. Meanwhile, they could see
Melodie the Music Fairy conducting the
musicians, and other fairies making
drinks and cooking food on a barbecue.

"The tide's coming in," Rachel
remarked to Jade as the
waves crept further up
the beach. "Will the
party be over soon?"

Jade shook her head.
"No, we're fine as long
as we stay above Party
Rock," she replied,

pointing to a large boulder next to them.

"But Shannon the Ocean Fairy can explain it better than I can."

A nearby fairy turned and smiled at the girls. She wore a peachy-pink skirt, a top of aquamarine ribbons and a glittering starfish clip in her hair.

"Hi, girls," said Shannon. "Jade's right. The sea never comes in beyond Party Rock, so we can enjoy the party all day long!"

"Great!" Rachel said happily.

A little while later, the girls were having fun dancing with their fairy friends when the music suddenly

stopped. Everyone turned to see
what had happened.

"Listen, please," called Shannon the
Ocean Fairy. "I'm afraid that the sea's
coming in too far!"

She pointed her wand at Party Rock
and everyone gasped in surprise. The
water was splashing around the base
of the rock, and the level was still rising!

"The water never comes in this far,"
Shannon declared anxiously.
"Something's wrong!"

High Tide

King Oberon frowned. "Maybe Jack
Frost is up to mischief again," he said.

Queen Titania nodded and turned
to Rachel and Kirsty. "Girls, would you
come back to the palace with us?"
she asked. "You might be able to help."

"Of course we will," Kirsty
and Rachel replied immediately.

Whenever Jack Frost and his goblins caused trouble in Fairyland, the girls helped the fairies put things right.

"And I'll explore my underwater world and see if I can find out why the sea is rising," Shannon said, diving neatly into the ocean.

Quickly, the other fairies began to clear the beach. Meanwhile, the King and Queen led Rachel and Kirsty back to the Fairyland palace.

"We'll go to the Royal Observatory," King Oberon said. "It's at the top of the tallest tower. The roof slides back so that our telescopes can view the night sky."

"And Cedric, our Royal Astronomer,

guards the Enchanted Pearls there,"
Queen Titania said as they climbed the
spiral staircase. "The pearls are magical,
and very important in Fairyland and in
your human world."

"Why?" Kirsty asked.

"The rosy-pink Dawn Pearl makes
sure that dawn comes each morning
so that the day can begin," the Queen
explained. "And it also affects the levels
of water in the oceans."

"The silver Twilight Pearl makes sure
that night falls every evening," the King
added. "And the final pearl is the
creamy-white Moon Pearl. It controls
the flow of water through the oceans
and the size of the waves." He sighed.
"I think something is wrong with the
Dawn Pearl, and that that's why the sea

is coming in so far."

Rachel and
Kirsty followed
the King and
Queen into the
observatory.
The room was
painted white,
but the sliding
roof, which
was closed,
was a deep
blue like
the night sky.
There were
large golden
telescopes,
and star charts
hung on the walls.

"Cedric!" Queen Titania exclaimed,
and the girls suddenly noticed a frog
footman sitting on the floor,
looking rather dazed.
He was wrapped
in a long velvet cloak
embroidered with
moons and stars.
"What happened?"
asked the Queen,
hurrying over to him.
"Are you all right?"
Cedric looked
very upset. He pointed
to a crystal box that was
lying open on the floor.
"Jack Frost and his goblins
have stolen the Enchanted
Pearls!" he told the Queen sadly.

"What?" King Oberon exclaimed,
horrified.

"Jack Frost again!"
Kirsty whispered
to Rachel.

"Let's see exactly
what happened,"
said Queen Titania,
and she pointed her wand upwards.

As magic from the Queen's wand
streamed across the ceiling, images
began to appear. There was Cedric,
studying a large chart, when a blast
of wind suddenly swept the door open
and in burst Jack Frost and a group
of goblins.

Shocked, Cedric leapt to his feet,
but Jack Frost pointed his wand at him.
Immediately an icy breeze shot towards

the footman, whirling
his cloak around him
and tying him up
in knots.

"Help!" Cedric
cried, as a fold
of the cloak wrapped
itself firmly around
his head. Jack Frost
smirked at him.
"Quickly, get the
Enchanted Pearls!"
he shouted to his
gang of goblins.

27

While Cedric struggled with his cloak,
three goblins rushed over to the crystal
box, flung back the lid and grabbed the
large, gleaming pearls: one pink, one
white and one silver. Throwing the box
carelessly to the floor, the goblins held
the pearls up triumphantly.

Jack Frost looked very pleased. "This
serves those horrible fairies right!"
he cried. "The King and Queen banned
me from the luau because I haven't been
behaving myself. Well, without the

Enchanted Pearls, their beach party
will be a washout!"

He laughed spitefully.
"There's going to be
mayhem in the
fairy and human
worlds with these
pearls missing.
Time and tides,
daybreak and
nightfall – all will
be disrupted!"

"Great idea,
master!" said one
of the goblins. "Where
shall we hide the pearls?"

"I'm fed up with the fairies
always finding the magic objects
we steal," Jack Frost said, thoughtfully.

"So, this time, we will hide the
pearls in the human world –
but underwater!"

The goblins looked
terrified. "But we can't
breathe underwater,"
they moaned.

"Fools!" Jack Frost said scornfully.
"My magic will soon sort that out."

He pointed his wand at the goblins
and a stream of large, icy bubbles flew from
its end. Each bubble floated down over one
of the goblins' heads like an old-fashioned
diving-helmet.

"Now you can breathe underwater,"
Jack Frost said. "And these…" he went on,
aiming his wand at the goblins' big green
feet, "will make you super-speedy
swimmers."

A burst of frosty sparkles swirled around the goblins' feet and, suddenly, they were all wearing huge black flippers.

Jack Frost looked sternly at the goblins. "Now, keep those Enchanted Pearls safe, or you'll have me to answer to!" he snapped. And, with another wave of his wand, a freezing wind sprang up and swept the goblins straight out of the window with the Enchanted Pearls.

Underwater World

"I'm sorry," Cedric said, as the pictures faded away.

"It's not your fault, Cedric," Queen Titania said gently.

"We must summon Shannon and tell her what has happened," King Oberon declared, waving his wand.

Seconds later, Shannon fluttered into

the observatory. "Your Majesties," she gasped, "My underwater world is in chaos! All the tides are wrong and it's upsetting the sea creatures."

"That's not surprising," King Oberon said grimly. "Jack Frost has stolen the three Enchanted Pearls and sent his goblins to hide them in the ocean in the human world."

Shannon looked horrified. "But that's going to affect the seas and daytime and night-time in the human world and in Fairyland!" she cried.

The Queen nodded. "It's up to you, Shannon," she said. "Do you think you can get the pearls back?"

"I'll do my best," Shannon replied.

"We'll help," Rachel said eagerly. "Won't we, Kirsty?"

"Of course," Kirsty agreed, "except that we can't breathe underwater."

Shannon grinned. "No problem, girls!"

She raised her wand and the girls saw two shiny bubbles stream towards them. They felt the bubbles settle over their heads, and then they heard a POP as the bubbles disappeared.

"Now you can breathe underwater," Shannon announced. "Let's go. There isn't a moment to lose!"

"Good luck," the Queen called as Shannon lifted her wand again. "And remember that the Enchanted Pearls will be much bigger in the human world!"

As magic sparkles from Shannon's wand cascaded down around them, Rachel and Kirsty shut their eyes.

"Welcome to my underwater world," Shannon laughed a moment later.

The girls opened their eyes. To their amazement, they were standing on the sandy golden seabed, surrounded by large shells and pink coral.

"We're under the sea!" Kirsty cried, and then clapped her hand to her mouth in astonishment. She was breathing and talking normally, as if she was on land. Strangely, the water didn't seem to feel wet, either.

"It's magical!" Rachel agreed, staring as a large fish with an amazing mane of stripy fronds swam past.

"That's a lionfish," Shannon explained. Then she put her head on one side, listening carefully.

The girls listened too and heard a strange barking sound, which gradually got louder and louder.

"Ah, now here are some friends who will help us find the goblins!" Shannon exclaimed happily, and, a moment later, a pack of sealions came racing through the water, their sleek black bodies twisting this way and that.

"Hello!" Shannon called.

The girls watched, enchanted, as the sealions bounced playfully around them, chattering and barking loudly. They reminded Rachel of a pack of friendly dogs.

Shannon spoke to the sealions,

then turned
to the girls.
"Follow me!"
she called.

Shannon darted off
and Rachel and Kirsty
followed. As they whizzed
through the warm water,
Kirsty was fascinated by
the shoals of fish and the
inky coral caves.

"The sealions told me the goblins
are near this shipwreck site," Shannon
said, pointing at the remains of
a Spanish galleon on the sea floor.

"It's a very popular place for divers,
so we must find the goblins before
someone spots them!"

Rachel gasped as a woman's figure
loomed up out of the sand in front of
her. "Oh, it's a ship's figurehead!"
she said, touching the peeling paint.

Just then, Kirsty's eye was caught
by a glint of gold on the seabed.

"That's a gold coin!" she said excitedly, pointing. "Look how brightly it's shining. There's lots of light around here."

"I know why that is," Shannon replied. "This isn't normal sunlight. It's the magical dazzle of the Dawn Pearl!"

"Ssh!" Rachel hissed suddenly, putting her finger to her lips. "I can hear goblin voices!"

Shannon, Rachel and Kirsty quickly swam behind a rock and then peeped out cautiously. A moment later, three goblins came swimming towards them – and one was carrying the Dawn Pearl.

A Treasure Trail

Rachel and Kirsty caught their breath as they gazed at the pearl. It was a beautiful rose-pink colour, and it shone with a dazzling brightness that filled the ocean with light.

Shannon and the girls watched as the goblins suddenly shot forward, their magic flippers propelling them quickly through the water.

"They're very fast swimmers with those flippers," Shannon whispered. "We won't be able to catch them if we have to give chase!"

The goblins began to swim around the wreck of the Spanish galleon, holding the pearl out in front of them.

"They're using the pearl like a torch!" Shannon frowned. "I hope none of the human divers around here spot the light."

"The goblins are looking for something," whispered Kirsty.

"There's no treasure here!" the biggest goblin exclaimed in disgust. "Let's look somewhere else."

The goblins moved away from the galleon and along the seabed. Shannon and the girls followed.

"Look, a treasure chest!" the smallest goblin squealed, pointing at a tarnished silver chest, half-buried in the sand. He swam down and heaved the lid back. Then he gave a shriek of fear as a shoal of brightly coloured fish swam out.

The other goblins roared with laughter.

Shannon grinned too, but then her face fell. "Oh, no!" she cried. "Girls, this is terrible!"

Rachel and Kirsty looked puzzled.

"Do you see that cleft in the rocks over there?" Shannon whispered, pointing at a narrow opening in a nearby rock wall.

The cleft was surrounded by vibrant blue and green seaweed and amazingly bright pink sea anemones.

"That's the entrance to the Mermaid Kingdom," Shannon went on.

"You mean, mermaids are real?" Rachel gasped.

"Yes, but they're very secretive," Shannon explained. "They're scared of being discovered by humans and having their kingdom revealed. Imagine the fuss!"

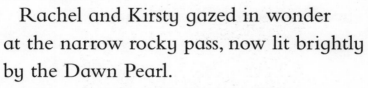

Rachel and Kirsty gazed in wonder at the narrow rocky pass, now lit brightly by the Dawn Pearl.

"If any divers come along now, they'll spot the goblins and maybe find the Mermaid Kingdom, too!" Shannon said anxiously.

Kirsty glanced at the goblins. Suddenly an idea popped into her head. "Maybe we can lure the goblins away with some treasure!" she exclaimed.

"If you could magic up some gold coins, Shannon, we could lay a trail for the goblins to follow."

"I can do that," Shannon agreed. "The magic coins won't last for ever, but they should stay long enough to fool the silly goblins."

"We could trap them in one of the coral caves we saw on the way here," Kirsty went on.

"Good idea," Rachel said eagerly. "With the goblins trapped, maybe we can get the Dawn Pearl back."

"And I know just how we can trap them!" Shannon declared eagerly. "I'll be back in a moment, girls."

And, with that, she swam quickly away, returning a few seconds later. "I've asked some friends for help," she explained, winking at the girls.

"Now, let me magic up a trail of gold!"

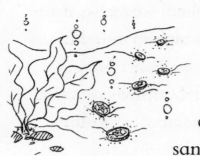

She waved her wand and the girls saw a trail of shiny coins appear in the sand, leading into a nearby coral cave.

"I hope the goblins spot them," Shannon whispered as the three friends hid inside the Spanish galleon.

The goblins were still swinging the Dawn Pearl this way and that, searching for treasure. Suddenly, one of the goblins gave a shriek of triumph as he spotted a coin glinting in the sand.

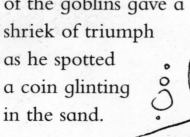

"Treasure!" he yelled, scooping it up.

Shannon and the girls grinned at each other.

"I see another one!" the biggest goblin shouted, dashing forward to grab a second coin.

Shannon, Rachel and Kirsty swam silently after the excited goblins as they picked up the gold coins, one by one. Kirsty held her breath as the goblins paused outside the cave.

Would they go in?

In the Coral Cave

To Kirsty's relief, the goblins hurried inside the coral cave.

"Let's go!" Shannon whispered, and she and the girls swam over to the cave mouth. Inside, the goblins were scrabbling around on the sandy floor, looking for more coins.

Shannon cleared her throat loudly.
The goblins shrieked with surprise.

"Please give me the Dawn Pearl,"
Shannon said politely.

"No way!" the goblins snorted.

"We're not letting you leave until
you do," Rachel told them.

"You silly little fairies can't stop us!"
the biggest goblin declared, moving
defiantly towards the girls, followed
by his friends.

Just as the girls were wondering what
to do, they heard a snapping sound.

Looking down, they saw an army of
lobsters scuttling into the cave and
snapping at the goblins' ankles with
their claws. The goblins screeched
in dismay and backed away.

"We can't stop you," Shannon agreed,
"but my lobster friends can. And they'll
snap at your ears
and noses too if
you don't give back
the Dawn Pearl."

The goblins
looked annoyed,
but they screamed
in fear when the
lobsters scuttled
towards them
again.

"OK," the biggest goblin squeaked. "It's yours!"

The goblins tossed the Dawn Pearl across the cave and Shannon, Rachel and Kirsty caught it between them.

"Thank you," Shannon called. "And thank you, my lobster friends."

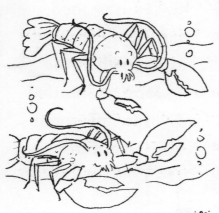

She waved her wand and a burst of fairy dust swept Rachel and Kirsty out of the water in an instant.

Blinking as the magic dust cleared, the girls realised that they were back on the beach in Leamouth.

"And we're not even wet," Kirsty said, looking down at her dry clothes.

"That's fairy magic!" Shannon laughed. She tapped the tip of her wand on the Dawn Pearl and it immediately shrank to its Fairyland size.

Then another sparkling shower of fairy dust made Kirsty and Rachel return to their normal sizes once again.

"I must take the
Dawn Pearl back
to Fairyland
now," Shannon
said. "Thank you
for all your help,
but we still have a
difficult task ahead
of us. We must find the
other two Enchanted Pearls!"

Rachel and Kirsty nodded and waved,
and their fairy friend blew them a kiss, and
then disappeared with the Dawn Pearl in
a whirl of fairy magic.

Trouble at
Sea

Contents

Ship Ahoy   65

Dolphins in the Dark   77

Grumbling Goblins   89

A Light in the Dark   99

From Twilight to Sunshine   107

Ship Ahoy

"It's another gorgeous day, Rachel!"
said Kirsty. "What shall we do?"

It was the following morning,
and the girls were getting ready
to go out with Kirsty's gran.

"I don't mind," Rachel replied.
She glanced across at Gran, who
was tidying the kitchen, and lowered
her voice.

"Maybe we helped to make the day start so bright and sunny by finding the Dawn Pearl."

"Maybe," Kirsty agreed. "I just hope we get a chance to help Shannon look for the other missing pearls today."

"What about a walk to the pier this morning, girls?" Gran suggested.

"That's a great idea!" Kirsty exclaimed. "There's a fairground at the end of the pier with a rollercoaster ride that goes right out over the sea!"

"Ooh, fun!" Rachel said with a grin.

Gran laughed. "Come on, then,"
she said.

They all set off along the seafront
towards the pier.

"Look at that big cruiseliner out at
sea," Gran remarked, as they passed
the harbour.

Rachel and Kirsty looked out across
the water to see a huge white ship with
black funnels in the distance.

"I don't suppose
it will be stopping
at Leamouth,"
Gran went on.
"Those big ships
never dock here."

"Look, Rachel, there's the old
lighthouse," Kirsty said. "There are
some really dangerous rocks around
the harbour, so the lighthouse was built
to guide ships in safely."

Rachel stared up at the white- and red-painted lighthouse standing on a rocky outcrop at the harbour entrance. "Is it still working?" she asked.

Gran shook her head. "No, modern ships have all sorts of high-tech equipment to guide them these days," she replied. "There are plans to turn it into an artists' studio."

They walked on towards the pier, at the other end of the beach.

"I expect you girls want to explore," Gran said as they reached the entrance. "I'll have a drink in the café while I'm waiting for you."

Gran led the way to The Starfish Café, a little way along the pier, and sat down at a table looking out over the sea.

"A pot of tea for one, please,"
Gran told the waiter.

The man wrote
it on his notepad.
"See that big
cruiseliner out
there?" he said
chattily. "It's
called *Seafarer,*
and they've just said on the local
radio station that it's going to dock
right here in Leamouth!"

"Really?" Gran asked, looking
surprised. "That's unusual."

"Yes, apparently the ship is
having problems with its navigation
systems and so it needs to dock
as soon as possible," the man explained.

"You'll have a perfect view of it from

this table, although it won't be docking
for an hour or so yet."

"It'll be brilliant to see the ship
coming in," Rachel commented.

Gran checked her watch. "Well, why
don't you go and explore, and then
come back to watch the ship dock?"
she suggested. "I'll sit here and read till
you get back," she added, taking a book
out of her handbag.

"See you later then, Gran," said
Kirsty, and she and Rachel set off
along the pier.

"The sky looks very black over there by the harbour entrance, even though the sun's shining," Rachel remarked, pointing far out to sea.

Kirsty nodded. "Maybe there's a storm coming," she replied.

The girls were just passing a small games arcade, when a machine by the entrance started flashing its lights and playing a merry tune.

Rachel stopped. "'FREE PLAY,'" she read aloud from the little screen.

"Have a go!" Kirsty urged.

"I've tried this before but I'm no good at it," Rachel admitted.

The machine was
full of soft toys in
a glass case, and a
large metal claw
hung above them.
The claw, which
was used to grab the
toys, was operated by a
lever. Rachel took hold of the lever and
moved the claw downwards. It swung
around a bit, but Rachel finally
managed to grab a fluffy dolphin.

"Well done!" Kirsty
cried, as Rachel carefully
moved the dolphin over
to the chute and released
the metal claw. The
dolphin dropped
straight down the chute.

"You did it!" Kirsty laughed.

Smiling, Rachel drew back the panel to retrieve her prize, then gasped as a cloud of aquamarine sparkles burst out.

"Hello, girls!" Shannon the Ocean Fairy cried. "I need your help to find the Twilight Pearl – and fast!"

Dolphins in the Dark

Rachel and Kirsty were keen to help.
"You'll have to be fairy-sized,"
Shannon said. "Quick, get out of sight."
Rachel and Kirsty ducked swiftly
behind the machine, where one flick
of Shannon's wand transformed
them into fairies, complete with
glittering wings.

Once again, Shannon conjured up magic bubbles to enable the girls to breathe underwater.

"Let's go, girls," Shannon said, flying off towards the end of the pier. Rachel and Kirsty whizzed after her.

"Nightfall is already being disrupted in parts of the world because the Twilight Pearl is missing," Shannon explained as they flew. "Last night, darkness didn't fall at the South Pole – luckily, only the penguins noticed!"

"There aren't any people living at the South Pole, are there?" asked Rachel.

"No, there aren't," Shannon replied, "so no humans have noticed the disruption yet. But if the Twilight Pearl isn't restored to its proper place soon, there'll be night-time chaos everywhere!"

"Where are the goblins with the Twilight Pearl?" Kirsty asked.

"I think they're underwater somewhere near here," Shannon replied. The presence of the Twilight Pearl is causing darkness to fall near the entrance to Leamouth Harbour."

"So that's why it's so dark!"
Rachel said, as they reached the
end of the pier. "We thought there
was a storm coming."

"Follow me!" Shannon called
as she plunged downwards
into the sparkling blue sea.

Rachel and Kirsty dived
beneath the waves after
her. As they sank deeper,
the sun filtered down
through the water,
lighting up the
golden seabed
and rippling
fronds of
seaweed.
A shoal of
silvery fish

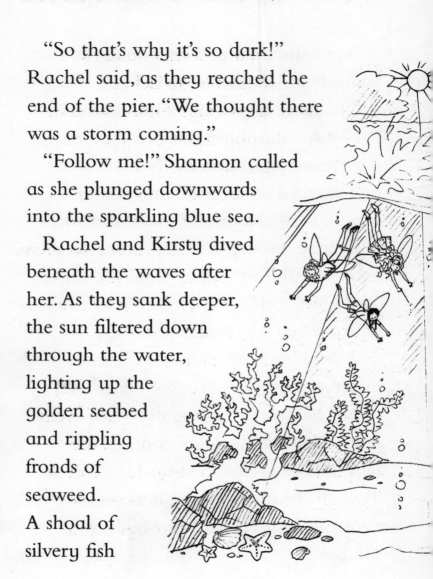

flickered past them and the
girls grinned in delight.

"This way," Shannon said,
darting through the greeny-
blue water.

Rachel and Kirsty
followed until Shannon
stopped and turned to them.

"Look, girls," she said,
"can you see how the
colour of the sea
is changing?"

Rachel and Kirsty
gazed ahead of them.
Sure enough, the
greeny-blue colour
of the water was
deepening to a
dark indigo.

"This is the effect of the Twilight Pearl," Shannon explained. She tapped her wand lightly on her hand, caught a sparkle as it fell and then fixed it to the tip of her wand, where it glowed brightly. "We'll use this to light our way. I just hope the goblins don't spot us coming."

Shannon swam off more slowly this time, with Kirsty and Rachel close behind her. But although Shannon's glowing wand helped a little, the waters around them were steadily growing darker and darker. Kirsty wondered how they were ever going to find the goblins and the

Twilight Pearl in
the ever-increasing
gloom.

Suddenly,
Shannon stopped
again, tipping her head to
one side and listening. "There's
someone who can help us!"
she said eagerly. "Wait here and I'll
be back in two shakes of a fish's tail!"
And she shot off into the darkness.

Rachel and Kirsty waited hopefully.
Seconds later, Shannon came back.

"Look who I found," she
announced, holding
up her lighted wand.
Rachel and Kirsty
gasped, as, behind
Shannon, they saw

a whole school of beautiful
blue dolphins.

The dolphins were
very friendly.
They swam around
Rachel and Kirsty,
squeaking and
clicking a
greeting, and
nudging the girls
gently with their
long noses.

"The dolphins
know the oceans
better than anyone
else," Shannon explained.
"They're going to take us to
the goblins." She waved her sparkling
wand in the air. "And the dolphins have

offered to let us ride on their backs, so we'll get there even more quickly!"

"That's fantastic!" Rachel exclaimed.

"I've always wanted to swim with dolphins," Kirsty breathed as one swam over to her and squeaked, inviting her to climb aboard. Kirsty clambered carefully onto its sleek back, as Rachel and Shannon jumped onto their own dolphins.

"Make sure you hold on tight," Shannon called, grabbing onto her dolphin's fin. "When a dolphin swims fast, it's really fast!"

"I see what you mean!" Kirsty gasped, as her dolphin took off like a rocket.

Chattering happily to each other, the other dolphins followed. Rachel and Kirsty hung on tightly as they zipped through the darkening seas.

"This is fun!" Rachel called. "Woohoo!" she cheered as her dolphin leapt out of the water and glided through the air in a perfect arc before plunging beneath the waves again.

Soon it was so dark underwater that Shannon and the girls could hardly even see each other, but the dolphins were still sure of where they were going, so neither Rachel nor Kirsty felt scared.

Suddenly, the dolphins began to slow down. In the darkness, the girls could hear voices ahead. They exchanged a knowing glance.

"Goblins!" whispered Kirsty.

Grumbling Goblins

The dolphins began to circle the goblins while Shannon, Kirsty and Rachel kept very still, listening hard. The goblins sounded scared.

"Oh, I don't like the dark," one whimpered. "Eek! What was that?"

"Maybe it was a sea-monster," another moaned. "I can't see."

"Something just swam past me,"
cried a third. "And I think it was
an underwater Pogwurzel!"

"HELP!" all the goblins shouted.
"WE'RE LOST IN THE DARK!"

Rachel and Kirsty could dimly see
Shannon fixing another sparkle to her
wand. It fizzed like a firework, lighting
up the ocean around them.

The goblins
stared in
amazement
at the circling
dolphins.

"It's not a
Pogwurzel," one
goblin sneered. "It's just dolphins – and
pesky fairies!"

"Give the Twilight Pearl back, and
we'll rescue you from the dark," Shannon
offered. "We know you're scared."

"Rubbish!" the biggest goblin scoffed.
"We're not scared, and we're not giving
back the pearl."

"OK, then we'll
go – and I'll take
my light with me,"
Shannon said firmly.

"NO!" all the goblins shrieked at once. "Please stay," gabbled the biggest goblin, looking terrified. "But we can't give the pearl back."

"Why not?" asked Rachel.

"Well it's just that..." the big goblin said hesitantly.

"We hid it somewhere really safe," another goblin added.

"And now we can't find it!" said another, sheepishly.

"But we know it's under a really big rock," added the big goblin helpfully.

Shannon whipped her wand through the water. It briefly lit up the sea around them before fading away.

In that time, Rachel and Kirsty saw that the area was *full* of really big rocks!

Suddenly there was the booming sound of a ship's horn overhead. The goblins cried out with fear and clapped their hands over their ears.

"I think that must be *Seafarer's* horn," said Rachel. "It's coming to dock in Leamouth because its navigation systems aren't working properly."

Shannon turned pale. "*Seafarer* won't be able to find its way through the rocks in the darkness caused by the Twilight Pearl!" she exclaimed. "It might run aground!"

Rachel and Kirsty glanced at each other in horror.

Then Kirsty's gaze fell on the glowing tip of Shannon's wand and an idea took shape in

her mind. "The ship would be OK if it had a light to guide it, wouldn't it?" she pointed out. "Shannon, could your magic get the old lighthouse working again?"

Shannon looked excited. "I think it could," she said. "But we'll have to hurry." She glanced at the goblins. "Stay here and keep out of trouble!" she told them. "When I get the lighthouse working, you'll have some light down here."

She jumped off her dolphin, patted
its nose and then zoomed up towards
the surface.

Rachel and Kirsty said a quick
goodbye to their dolphins and followed.
They broke through the water and
shot up into the air, then gasped
in amazement.

The Twilight Pearl had made night fall, and the sky around them was velvety-black and spangled with stars that sparkled like diamonds. It was beautiful.

"There's *Seafarer*," Kirsty shouted, pointing at the faint silhouette of the ship near the harbour entrance.

"And look at all those rocks in its path!" Rachel added anxiously.

A Light in the Dark

"To the lighthouse, girls!" Shannon cried. She whizzed off at great speed through the blackness, and the girls zoomed after her.

"How are we going to get inside?" Rachel asked when they reached the lighthouse door, which was locked.

"There's a broken windowpane there," Shannon said, pointing upwards.

She led the way up to the window and into the dark lighthouse. It smelt dusty and damp as the fairies flew up the spiral staircase to the very top of the tower. Here was the huge lantern, surrounded by mirrors to reflect the light out to sea. "Look, the bulb's broken!" Rachel exclaimed, pointing at the lantern.

"The electricity has
probably been switched
off, anyway," said Kirsty.
"It hasn't been used
in years."

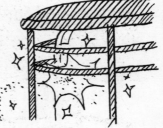

"My fairy
magic can fix it,"
Shannon replied,
pointing her wand
at the lantern.
"But my spell won't
last for ever. I just
hope it's long enough
for *Seafarer* to dock safely."

Rachel and Kirsty watched
as a stream of sparkles flew from
Shannon's wand and surrounded
the lantern.

With many loud creaks and groans, the lantern began to turn. Slowly, too, the broken bulb began to glow, getting brighter and brighter.

"It's lighting up the sea for miles!" Kirsty cheered. "Look, it's showing up all the rocks around the harbour mouth."

As the three friends watched, *Seafarer* began to make its way into the harbour. And then Rachel noticed something odd: every time

the lantern's beam fell on a particular
place in the ocean, she could see a
strange, silvery-grey shimmer in
the water.

"Thank goodness," said Shannon,
once *Seafarer* had cleared the rocks.
"Now we'd better see what those
naughty goblins are up to."

She zoomed over to the window
and Kirsty followed. But Rachel
hesitated, waiting for the light
to fall on the same patch
of water once more.

103

"Shannon, look over there!" Rachel cried, pointing as the sea glittered silvery-grey. "Could the Twilight Pearl be there, underwater?"

Shannon looked where Rachel was pointing and then clapped her hands in delight. "It *is* the Twilight Pearl, I'm sure of it!" she declared.

"Well done, Rachel," Kirsty added.

Swiftly, the three friends whizzed out of the lighthouse, heading straight towards the glittering patch of sea.

As they plunged down into the water, they were bathed in an eerie silver light that shimmered all around them.

"There it is!" Kirsty exclaimed, spotting the Twilight Pearl lying beneath a large rock. She gazed at it in wonder. The pearl's unusual, silvery sheen was truly magical.

But suddenly, to Kirsty's horror, a goblin swam sneakily round from the other side of the rock and grabbed the Twilight Pearl!

From Twilight to Sunshine

As Shannon and the girls watched in dismay, all the other goblins appeared.

"Oh, no," Rachel groaned. "The beam from the lighthouse has helped the goblins find the pearl, too!"

"We'll have that, please," said Kirsty, holding out her hands. But the goblins just laughed.

"Go away!" jeered one. "The pearl belongs to us!"

"If you don't give us that pearl right now," Shannon said, looking very fierce, "I'll turn the lighthouse off again and leave you here. You know how Pogwurzels love the dark!" And she winked at the girls.

The goblins looked panic-stricken. "Take the pearl. Take the pearl!" they gabbled, pushing it through the water to the fairies and swimming speedily away.

Laughing, Shannon touched her wand to the Twilight Pearl. It shrank

immediately, and she swept it up into
her arms, spinning round in delight.

"Everyone in Fairyland will be so
pleased to have the Twilight Pearl

returned," she cried. "But,
girls, you must get back
to Kirsty's gran so
that you can watch
Seafarer come into dock."

The three friends flew
quickly to the deserted
end of the pier, where
Shannon soon restored
Kirsty and Rachel to
their human size.

"We just have the Moon Pearl to find
now," Shannon reminded the girls as she
gave them a quick hug. "See you again
very soon!"

And she vanished
in a cloud of fairy
dust.

   Rachel and
Kirsty hurried
back down the
pier. As they passed
the arcade, Kirsty
noticed that the toy dolphin Rachel
had won was still lying in the chute of
the machine.

"Look, here's your dolphin," Kirsty said, handing it to Rachel.

"Let's share it," Rachel suggested. "It'll remind us of our fantastic underwater adventures!"

Kirsty nodded and the girls ran back to the café, where lots of people had gathered to watch *Seafarer* approach.

"Ah, there you are, girls," said Gran. "I was worried a storm was brewing; it was so dark out at sea. But luckily someone's managed to get the old lighthouse working to guide *Seafarer* in."

Rachel and Kirsty shared a secret smile.

The huge cruiseliner was moving slowly into the harbour now. As it did so, the darkness began to lift and the sun came out. Everyone clapped and cheered as the ship docked safely.

"Look, the lighthouse is dark again, now," Kirsty whispered. "Shannon's fairy magic kept it working just long enough!"

"And the Twilight Pearl is safely back in Fairyland," Rachel added happily. "Now, I wonder where the goblins have hidden the Moon Pearl..."

Contents

Message in a Bottle   119

Flooding in Fairyland   125

Weird Waves   133

Seahorses Save the Day   147

The Tide Turns   159

Message in a Bottle

"Oh, dear!" Gran exclaimed as she read the paper.

"What's the matter, Gran?" asked Kirsty. It was the following morning, and the girls were getting ready to go down to the beach.

"There are reports of major floods in coastal areas all around the world," Gran explained.

"Apparently the sea is behaving very strangely, and the high tides are coming in much further than they usually do."

Rachel and Kirsty glanced at each other in concern. They knew that this was because the Moon Pearl, which controlled the tides, was missing from Fairyland.

"Have fun at the beach, girls, but make sure you're back for lunch," Gran went on. "And just keep an eye out for the tides, although Leamouth doesn't seem too badly affected at the moment."

"OK," the girls agreed.

"I wonder if Shannon's found out where the goblins are hiding with the

Moon Pearl," Rachel said as they hurried through the garden and down the cliff steps to the beach.

"I hope she has," Kirsty replied. "All those floods sound scary!"

It was still early so the beach was deserted. The girls decided to go straight down to the sea and paddle. Removing their flip-flops, they waded into the cool, clear water.

"Isn't it funny to think we were actually under the sea yesterday?" Kirsty remarked.

Rachel was about to reply when her eye was caught by a green glass bottle bobbing up and down on the waves. It had a cork in the top, and, with a rush of excitement, Rachel realised that there was a piece of paper inside.

"Kirsty, look at this," she called, grabbing the bottle as it floated past her. "It's a message in a bottle."

Kirsty paddled over and peered through the glass at the piece of paper. "It says 'Open me!'" she read aloud.

Rachel smiled broadly. "Let's see what happens," she said, pulling out the cork.

Immediately, a sparkling mist of
aquamarine dust burst out of the bottle –
and so did Shannon the Ocean Fairy!

Flooding in Fairyland

"Girls, I need your help!" Shannon declared, looking very pale. "Fairyland is flooding fast!"

"Oh, no!" Rachel exclaimed.

"Is everyone safe?" Kirsty asked.

Shannon shook her head. "The toadstool houses are being flooded," she explained. "Fairyland is in chaos!"

"How can we help?" asked Rachel.

"We must find the Moon Pearl without delay," Shannon replied. "And I think I know where the goblins who have it are hiding."

"Where?" asked Rachel.

"Hawaii!" Shannon told her.

"Hawaii?" Kirsty repeated, amazed. "How are we going to get there?"

"With fairy magic, of course!" Shannon laughed. Quickly she waved her wand and turned the girls into sparkling fairies. Once she had conjured up some magic bubbles too, so that the girls could breathe underwater, they were ready to go.

"Follow me," Shannon said, diving neatly into the waves.

Kirsty and Rachel did the same.

"Now, stay very close to me," Shannon instructed, linking arms with the girls and waving her wand again.

Rachel and Kirsty let out a gasp as they were suddenly swept off their feet at top speed. The three friends were carried through the water by a magic current, their hair streaming out behind them.

They were going so fast that the girls couldn't see anything except for swirls of rainbow-coloured bubbles that were also swept along on the stream of magic.

A few minutes later the girls felt themselves slowing down.

"That was like a super-fast rollercoaster ride!" Rachel exclaimed in delight as she caught her breath.

Kirsty nodded. "The water feels much warmer here," she remarked.

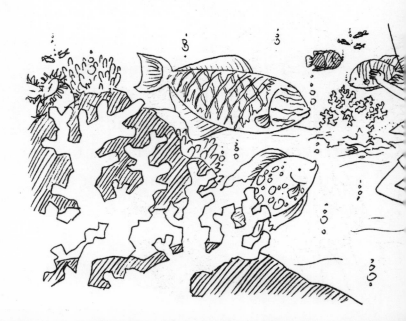

"That's because we're in Hawaii,"
Shannon declared. "See the coral reef?"

Rachel and Kirsty gazed around.
The sea was a clear sapphire-blue and
there were all kinds of colourful tropical
fish weaving their way through the reef
of pink, red and white coral. The sun
shone through the water, creating pretty
patterns on the seabed.

"It's like an underwater garden,"
Kirsty breathed.

"Let's go and see what the goblins
are up to," Shannon said with a grin.
"I think they're up here." She zoomed
upwards and the girls followed.

Peeping out of the water, Rachel and
Kirsty saw a beautiful island nearby with
palm trees and a golden, sandy beach.

"Listen," Shannon whispered.

Rachel and Kirsty suddenly realised that they could hear shouts and whoops of glee. They turned and saw a big, rolling wave making its way towards the beach. And riding on top of the wave, on brightly coloured surfboards, was a group of giggling goblins.

Weird Waves

Rachel, Kirsty and Shannon had to muffle their laughter as they watched the goblins surfing. They all had garlands of flowers around their necks and some were wearing flowery Hawaiian shirts or long grass skirts.

"They look so funny!" Rachel laughed. "But aren't they supposed to be in hiding with the Moon Pearl?"

"I think they've forgotten about that,"
Shannon replied. "They're having so
much fun!"

"These waves are enormous," Kirsty
remarked as another huge wall of water
headed towards the beach. "They're
perfect for surfing."

Shannon nodded.

"Yes, that's what Hawaii's famous for,"
she said. "But these waves are even
bigger than usual!" She frowned. "I think

the goblins are using the Moon Pearl to
make the waves bigger. And to do that,
they must have the Moon Pearl
underwater and close at hand."

"Let's start searching!" Kirsty said
eagerly.

The others nodded and the three
friends ducked under the water again.

As Rachel and Kirsty looked
around for any sign of the Moon Pearl,
they suddenly spotted a group of bright
blue seahorses bobbing through the
water towards them.

The tiny seahorses swam right up
to Shannon and started talking to her
in bubbly, high-pitched, little voices.

"Aren't they cute?" Kirsty said.
"I wonder what they're saying."

Shannon grinned and waved her wand,
and Rachel and Kirsty suddenly found
that they could understand the seahorses.

"Hello, Shannon," the little seahorses chorused. "Hello, girls."

"We're very pleased to meet you," said one.

"Yes, very pleased to meet you," the others repeated.

Rachel and Kirsty were enchanted. "We're very pleased to meet you, too," they replied.

"These baby seahorses are friends of mine," Shannon explained. "I've known them ever since they were born."

"Yes, ever since we were born!" the seahorses chorused in agreement.

"Ever since we were born!" squeaked another one, a little behind his friends.

"We're looking for the Moon Pearl," Shannon told them. "Have you seen it?"

The seahorses bounced up and down in the water, looking very excited. "We think so! We think so!" they all yelled in their tiny voices.

"Not far from here are two strange green creatures," one of the seahorses explained.

"They've got flappy black feet."

"Flappy black feet!" the others repeated.

"And they're guarding a big, white pearl," another added.

"A BIG WHITE PEARL!" shouted all the seahorses together.

"They were over there by a tall, pointy rock, next to the coral reef," one seahorse explained.

"Over there, over there!" chorused the others.

"Thank you, my dears," Shannon said with a smile. "Come on, girls."

She swam off at speed, and Kirsty and
Rachel followed, pausing only to wave
at the seahorses, who were swimming up
and down in a frenzy of excitement.

It didn't take long to find the rock the
seahorses had mentioned. Cautiously
Shannon and the girls peeped out from
behind it.

"There they are," Shannon whispered.
"And there's the Moon Pearl!"

Two goblins were playing catch
with a big, creamy-white pearl.

Kirsty caught her
breath in wonder,
watching the
pearl shimmer in
the turquoise water as
the goblins tossed it
back and forth.

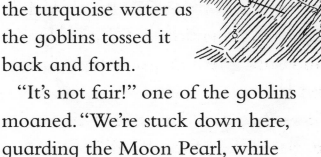

"It's not fair!" one of the goblins
moaned. "We're stuck down here,
guarding the Moon Pearl, while
everyone else is surfing."

"Yes, and two new guards were
supposed to come
and take over
after half an
hour," the
other grumbled.
"But nobody's
turned up!"

Shannon grinned at Rachel and Kirsty. "There are only two of them," she whispered. "This is our chance to get the pearl. But how?"

Rachel thought for a moment. "Maybe we could sneak over to the goblins and grab the pearl when it's in mid-air," she suggested. "Like in a game of piggy-in-the-middle."

142

Kirsty nodded. "There's coral and clumps of seaweed to hide behind," she said eagerly. "Let's give it a try."

The three of them swam silently from behind the rock to a boulder covered with colourful sea-anemones. Then they slipped through the gap between two large pieces of coral and hid behind a clump of seaweed. They were very close to the goblins now.

Anxiously, they all peered through the seaweed to see if the goblins had spotted them, but they were still throwing the pearl to and fro.

"OK, we're right between the goblins here," Shannon whispered. "Who's going to try to grab the pearl?"

"Rachel, you're good at ball games," said Kirsty.

"I'll have a go," Rachel agreed bravely.

They all waited as one of the goblins prepared to throw the pearl back to the other.

"Now, Rachel!" Shannon said.

Rachel soared upwards from behind the seaweed at the very moment that the goblin tossed the pearl. As it flew through the air, Rachel swam forward, stretching out her arms to grab it.

Kirsty held her breath as she watched. Would Rachel be able to reach the pearl before the goblins realised what was going on?

Seahorses Save the Day

Rachel felt her fingertips brush the surface of the pearl, but it was too high for her to catch. "Oh, no!" she groaned as the pearl flew over her head.

"It's those dratted fairies!" yelled the goblin who'd thrown the pearl.

With a determined look on his face,
the other goblin zoomed upwards with
the help of his flippers and snatched the
pearl before Rachel could try to grab
it again.

"Now, run away!" the first goblin
shouted. "Run away!"

The two goblins shot off, propelling
themselves at top speed with their huge

magic flippers. Quickly, Shannon
and Kirsty flew to join Rachel.

"After them!" Shannon gasped.

The three of them swam swiftly
after the goblins.

They raced along the coral reef,
passing shoals of fish and even a very
surprised-looking turtle. But the
goblins, with the help of their
magic flippers, were just
too quick to catch.

"It's no good," Shannon panted as the goblins disappeared from sight. "They're too fast."
She stopped and glanced at Rachel and Kirsty in dismay. "How are we ever going to get the Moon Pearl back?"

Suddenly they heard a chorus of tiny voices say, "We can help! We can help!" The little seahorses were back, bobbing through the water in a long line. "Let us help you catch the goblins!"

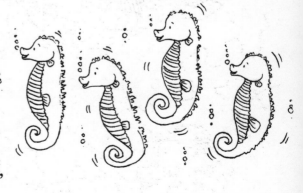

"You can ride on our backs,"
one suggested.

"You can ride on our backs!" the
others agreed.

Shannon smiled. "That's very kind,"
she said gently, "but I don't think you'll
be fast enough."

"We will, we will," the seahorses
chorused. "We've been practising.
Now we're extra fast!"

Shannon turned to Rachel and Kirsty.

"In that case, climb aboard, girls,"
she laughed.

Rachel and Kirsty each jumped onto
the back of a seahorse, and Shannon
did the same.

"Hold on! Hold tight!" the seahorses
shouted and zoomed away.

"They are fast!" Kirsty gasped, clinging
to her seahorse's neck as they shot
through the water at great speed.

The seahorses were extremely agile,
dodging neatly around obstacles like
rocks and shells and racing in and out
of the coral arches.

"There are the goblins," Rachel said, as she caught a glimpse of them swimming just ahead. "We're catching them up!"

How are we ever going to get the pearl away from them? Kirsty wondered as the seahorses whizzed past a clump of feathery seaweed. But as she glanced at the long fronds waving in the water, she suddenly had an idea. "Maybe we could tie the goblins up with seaweed!"

"Good idea!" Shannon cried. She
immediately raised her wand, and,
with a burst of fairy magic, knotted
together some long strands of seaweed.

"Rachel, you take one end of the
seaweed rope," Shannon instructed,
"and if your seahorse keeps still
when we get near the goblins,
Kirsty and I can tie the goblins up."

"Yes, keep still, keep still," Rachel's
seahorse repeated, nodding his
little head.

Quietly, Rachel, Kirsty, Shannon
and the seahorses sneaked up behind
the goblins.

"Now, everyone except Rachel and
her seahorse whizz round and round
the goblins," Shannon whispered.

All the seahorses darted forwards,
except for Rachel's, who stayed very still.
Rachel hung on to one end of the rope,

while Kirsty and Shannon held the
rest of it.

"Hurrah!" the seahorses yelled
excitedly as they swam around the
goblins at top speed. "Round and
round and round we go!"

The Tide Turns

The goblins' eyes almost popped out of their heads when they saw Kirsty, Shannon and the seahorses racing around them.

"It's those fairies again!" one of them yelled. "Run for it!"

But before they could move, the seaweed rope tightened around them,

stopping them in their tracks. The goblins
cried out with rage as another and then
another length of the seaweed rope tied
them up in knots.

"Help!" the goblins shrieked.

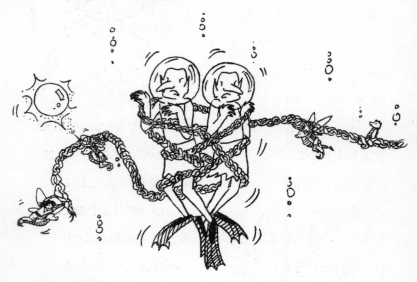

Rachel, Kirsty and Shannon rode their
seahorses over to the goblins and took
the Moon Pearl right out of their hands.
The goblins scowled at them.

"When we let go of the rope, it will take you a little while to free yourselves," Shannon told them. 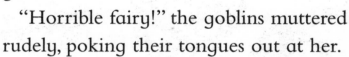 "That will give you time to think about how naughty you've been."

"Horrible fairy!" the goblins muttered rudely, poking their tongues out at her.

 Shannon quickly touched her wand to the creamy surface of the Moon Pearl, and it instantly shrank to its Fairyland size.

"Thank you, my friends," Shannon called to the seahorses, who were still dancing happily around the goblins. She waved her wand, showering herself and Rachel and Kirsty with sparkles. "See you again soon!"

"Bye-bye! Bye-bye!" the seahorses chorused.

The next moment, the girls found themselves whizzing through the air as Shannon's

magic whisked them up
and out of the sea.

"I think the goblins will rush
back to Jack Frost now to tell
him they've lost the Moon Pearl,"
Shannon called
to Rachel and Kirsty.

"Which means that hopefully
they'll leave Hawaii before
any humans spot them."
She glanced down
and pointed with her
wand. "Look, girls!"
Rachel and Kirsty
gazed down and saw
that they
were now
flying over
Fairyland.

Rachel gasped.
"Look at the
river!" she cried.

The twisting river
that wound its way
through the green fairy
meadows had burst
its banks. Lots of the
toadstool houses
were already
surrounded
by water.

"Fairyland is even more badly affected
than the human world, because
everything's so small," Shannon said.
Kirsty and Rachel were dismayed
to see that the pink and white
Fairyland palace was also flooded.

Shannon swooped down and in through the window of the Royal Observatory, with the girls right behind her.

Inside, they found King Oberon, Queen Titania and Cedric the Royal Astronomer.

"Ah, we knew you wouldn't let us down," King Oberon declared with a smile as Shannon handed the Moon Pearl to Cedric.

Cedric beamed as he hurried over to the crystal box.

He placed the Moon Pearl next to the Dawn and Twilight Pearls, and all three shimmered with a magical glow.

"Come and look out of the window, girls," said Queen Titania.

Kirsty and Rachel ran to see.

"The water level's going down already!" Kirsty cried, relieved.

They all watched happily as fairies began popping out of their little houses, cheering and clapping.

"This calls for a celebration!" Queen Titania proclaimed. "And what

better way to celebrate than to finish
our luau?"

Shannon and the girls glanced at each
other in delight as the Queen hurried
off to organise the party.

Soon the luau was in full swing on the
beach again. Kirsty, Rachel and all the
fairies joined in the singing and dancing.

"This is the best party ever," Rachel sighed happily as the sun began to set on Fairyland.

Just then, King Oberon called for attention. "We want to thank Shannon the Ocean Fairy and Rachel and Kirsty for saving Fairyland from flooding," he announced. "Without them, Jack Frost would still have our precious pearls."

The Queen pointed her wand at Rachel and Kirsty and a shower of fairy dust fell gently around them. When it cleared, the girls gasped with delight.

They were each wearing a beautiful gold ring set with a rosy pink pearl that looked just like the Dawn Pearl.

"Thank you," Rachel and Kirsty said gratefully.

"And now you must be getting home," said the Queen.

Shannon gave the girls a big hug. "Goodbye," she cried.

"Goodbye!" Rachel and Kirsty called, waving to all their friends as the Queen's magic sent them whizzing home.

A few seconds later, the girls found themselves on the beach near Gran's house, and back to their normal size once again.

"Wasn't that an amazing adventure?" Kirsty said happily as they went up the cliff steps towards the house.

"Oh, yes," Rachel agreed, admiring her beautiful ring. "Our fairy adventures are always amazing. But this one under the sea was extra special!"

**Now it's time for Kirsty and Rachel
to help...**

Poppy the Piano Fairy

Read on for a sneak peek...

"Ooh, I love to dance!" Rachel Walker
sang along to the radio, pretending her
hairbrush was a microphone. "When
I hear the music, my toes start tapping
and my fingers start snapping – I just
love to dance!"

Kirsty Tate, Rachel's best friend,
grinned and grabbed her own hairbrush.

"I can't stop dancing!" she chorused.
"Just can't stop dancing!"

The girls tried to do a complicated
dance routine as they sang but then
Kirsty went left and Rachel went right

and they ended up bumping into each other. Laughing, they collapsed onto Kirsty's bedroom carpet.

"It's really hard to sing and dance at the same time," said Rachel as the song ended.

"I know," Kirsty agreed. "I don't think we'd be very good in a band, Rachel!"

"That was The Sparkle Girls with their new single, 'Can't Stop Dancing'," the radio DJ announced as Kirsty and Rachel scrambled to their feet. "And if anyone out there thinks they could make it big as a pop star too, why not come along and audition for the National Talent Competition next weekend...?"

Read Poppy the Piano Fairy to find out
what adventures are in store for Kirsty and Rachel!

RAINBOW magic®

Meet the fairies, play games
and get sneak peeks at
the latest books!

www.rainbowmagicbooks.co.uk

There's fairy fun for everyone on
our wonderful website.
You'll find great activities, competitions, stories and
fairy profiles, and also a special newsletter.

Get 30% off all Rainbow Magic books at
www.rainbowmagicbooks.co.uk

Enter the code RAINBOW at the checkout.
Offer ends 31 December 2012.

Offer valid in United Kingdom and Republic of Ireland only.

Win Rainbow Magic Goodies!

There are lots of Rainbow Magic fairies, and we want to know
which one is your favourite! Send us a picture of her and tell
us in thirty words why she is your favourite and why you like
Rainbow Magic books. Each month we will put the entries into
a draw and select one winner to receive a Rainbow Magic
Sparkly T-shirt and Goody Bag!

Send your entry on a postcard to Rainbow Magic Competition,
Orchard Books, 338 Euston Road, London NW1 3BH.
Australian readers should email: childrens.books@hachette.com.au
New Zealand readers should write to Rainbow Magic Competition,
4 Whetu Place, Mairangi Bay, Auckland NZ.
Don't forget to include your name and address.
Only one entry per child.

Good luck!

Meet the Music Fairies